Euphoria

A Royal Love Story

Nikita Bhakhri

Copyright © 2013 Nikita Bhakhri
All rights reserved.

ISBN: 1-4819-3669-7
ISBN-13: 9781481936699

Dedication

To my parents, Vipan and Kusam Bhakri; to my siblings, Jyoti Sandhu and Abhi Bhakri; and to my brother-in-law, Triptej Sandhu. Words cannot express how thankful I am to have you all in my life. Your support is my greatest strength; I love you all. This novel is also dedicated to my friends, Pali Lalria and the late Sneha Malhotra. Thank you for believing in me and pushing me to do my best.

Prologue

Breena could see him standing in the staircase with his back toward her. She didn't know who he was, but he looked like a prince of some kind. But why couldn't she see his face? Every night since she was a child, she could sense him, but he was always a blur. He would never speak to her, he would never face her, but she could still sense his massive pull.

However, today was different because today she could see her surroundings, and she could see him. They were in a castle at what looked like a royal ball. He was looking up at someone, but at whom? Breena looked up and saw a girl who had her face, but it couldn't have been her. This girl was dressed in a royal gown, wearing a beautiful tiara; she seemed like some kind of princess.

The man looking up started speaking. "Mimi, hurry up; I'm waiting for my special dance."

With that, Breena opened her eyes and started to yawn; it was already morning. It seemed like she had just started to sleep, but that was okay because today was special for her. It was her sixteenth birthday, which meant she was going to be getting presents. But that didn't stop her from thinking about her dream. Breena wanted to know who that guy was and why she couldn't see his face. She wanted to know why that girl named Mimi looked like her duplicate. Above all she wanted to know why she was having dreams about them.

Yet, there was something else that was different about this morning. From the moment she had woken up, she had heard a deep male voice in her head; but this voice seemed so familiar. Nevertheless Breena didn't want to stress herself out by thinking about her dream or the voice. Instead she turned around and started going through her drawer to find her personal diary.

Dear Diary:

Guess what? Today is my sixteenth birthday. I'm so excited to find out what my family got me; usually they give off clues, but this year there's been absolutely nothing. All my mother keeps telling me is how destiny works in weird ways and that no one really knows what will happen in their life because free will is just an illusion. Then Papa Bear starts explaining how trust can sometimes be misleading because of hidden secrets. But, c'mon, let's be real. Those can't be clues, because that just doesn't make any sense. To be honest I just hope they finally got me a car. I mean, I'm tired of taking the bus to school. Oh, yeah, a few other things happened today; I had that dream again, but today I saw him from behind. Afterwards when I woke up, I had this feeling that someone—well, that some guy, to be more precise—was calling out to me.

It sounded like he was wishing me a happy birthday and trying to explain something serious to me—as if he was giving me a heads-up. I don't know how to explain what was going on, but it felt like he was pulling me closer to himself. For some odd reason, his voice sounded so familiar; it was deep and soothing. I know I sound like a weirdo right now, but I think I fell in love with his voice. Maybe he's just the prince of my dreams. Hopefully I'll meet him one day. If I don't, then I hope that I'll be fortunate enough to hear his voice again. I don't even know if I'm the proper age to be having feelings like this, but I can't help it. I just feel such a strong attraction to this person's voice.

It seems like I've known him for so long. I didn't even see his face, but I could feel his warmth and sense his heartbeats; I know all of this couldn't have been in my head. Perhaps hearing his voice was a sign from God that I should start preparing myself to meet the person of my dreams. As my mom says, "Destiny works in unusual ways." Well, I have to go downstairs now; my mother is calling me. I guess guests have started coming over. I didn't even know that we were having a birthday party for me, but I did hear the doorbell ringing. I really have to go check it out, so I shall write in you tomorrow. Happy sixteenth birthday to me!

Sincerely,

Breena Faylinn

Chapter One:
Secret Revealed

"My sweet little birthday girl, can you please come downstairs? We need to discuss something very important with you, darling," said Mrs. Eve Faylinn.

Breena made her way down the stairs to see her parents and two young boys sitting in her living room.

"IT'S MY BIRTHDAY! YES IT IS, YES IT IS! But wait, if you don't mind me asking, who are our guests?" asked Breena.

"Happy birthday, Princess. Thank you for finally joining us. We need to talk about your heritage, your future, and, most of all, about you. So could you please take a seat?" said Mr. Aristo Faylinn.

2

Breena didn't understand what was going on but decided to take a seat before her father lost his temper. She then asked, "Can you please explain why we need to talk about those things all of the sudden? And why do all of you look so tense?"

Finally, after a short while, her father spoke again.

"Breena, remember when you were little and you would ask me what your full name meant? Then I would say, 'I'll tell you when the time's right.' Well, I think that time has finally arrived. The meaning of Breena is 'fairyland,' and the meaning of Faylinn is 'fairy kingdom.' Once you add those two together, you get your name, Breena Faylinn, meaning, the fairy kingdom within the fairyland. I know this will sound absurd, but, darling, you're the princess of my homeland—the next in line to sit on the throne and rule over Euphoria, our fairyland."

Breena couldn't believe her ears; she had to say something before her father continued. "Papa Bear, I'm sorry for interrupting, but I just have to make this clear for myself. So you're telling me that I'm Princess Breena Faylinn of Euphoria, which happens

3

to be a place I've never even heard of, and that I'm a fairy? A *FAIRY*? Please, tell me this is some type of silly joke you're playing with me. I mean, how can I be a fairy? If I was a fairy, wouldn't I have wings? Be able to fly? And, I don't know...have magic? How is any of that even possible? And another thing: if I'm a princess, shouldn't I be living in some type of castle or something?"

"Breena calm down. This is the reality. You're the next descendent of the Faylinn family, who happens to be the ruling royal family in Euphoria. You are a fairy. However, you're not a full-fledged fairy, but an elemental fairy. This means you're half human and half fairy—the second of your kind in the history of Euphoria. The reason you've never heard of Euphoria is because it isn't part of this world exactly. You see, its part of Selectum, which is a world connected to Earth through the Bermuda Triangle. I guess you could say it's a parallel universe. The reason we don't live there right now is because your grandfather, King Faylinn, wanted me to marry a royal pixrie, but I was in love with your mother. So he gave me two choices: listen to him and marry the girl he chose, or marry Eve and get kicked out; therefore, I chose Eve, your mother. In spite of that he said my firstborn would be

4

the next to sit on the throne after him, and I would never get the chance to rule over my country."

Breena still didn't understand any of the information she was getting. Until now her world consisted of worrying about getting her homework done on time and dealing with being a normal teenager. But this information was out of the ordinary. What sixteen-year-old gets the gift of being a princess for her birthday? It just didn't make sense to her. She decided to ask more questions to get a better understanding of what her dad was telling her.

"Alright, so I'm a princess, and I'm an elemental fairy of Euphoria, Selectum? Where are your wings? Where are my wings? Why are you telling me all of this now? And could you please tell me who those two boys are?"

"I think you understand what I'm saying. I'll show you my wings in a little while and explain how you get yours. The reason I'm telling you all of this is because your grandfather is very sick now, and he only has a limited time to live. So he has sent these two young boys to get you and has asked me to explain the *Cryptoria* to you. See, the *Cryptoria* is our land's ancestry book; it contains all the

5

secrets, history, and prophecies of Euphoria.
It's our family's job to keep it safe, because
another land named Felicity is after it. And
now since your grandfather is on the verge of
passing away, they're planning on attacking
Euphoria to get the *Cryptoria* and rule over
our land. Euphoria has tried to make peace
with them over and over again, but they insist
on war. Now the only way things will be
solved is after the war. Either Euphoria gets
the *Cryptolicity*, which is their ancestry book,
or Felicity gets the *Cryptoria*.

"So you have to go there and learn
about your proper heritage and about how
to run our country. I'm passing down the
Cryptoria to you, but you have to promise me that you'll keep it safe and never
let anyone touch it or even see it, for that
matter. Only the people in your family
or someone you really trust should see it;
never show it to any stranger. Remember
what I told you. Everyone has their own
secret, so never trust anyone too quickly.
Now for my wings," said Prince Faylinn
as he popped out his glorious wings that
stunned Breena.

She had never even thought she would
see such beautiful wings colored navy blue
and gold.

6

She couldn't wait any longer, so once again she said to her father, "OMG. OMG. OMG. I want my wings too. Alright, so I'm supposed to go to Euphoria with these two strangers? And are you both going to be coming with me, or am I supposed to go by myself? And I promise I'll keep the *Cryptoria* safe no matter what. So now whenever the war happens, I'll make sure our army gains the *Cryptolicity*."

Breena's answer pleased Eve and Aristo, so Aristo decided to tell his daughter how to get her wings and about who those two guys actually were. "Well, you'll get your magic once you start attending Spirits of the Air High School. And for your wings, you need to close your eyes, really believe in yourself, and repeat after me: Ek orin di. Do orin di. Snip snap. Fling flung. Up, down, left, right. The ones I've wanted, the ones I've sought. Come to me. Ek orin di. Do orin di."

And that's exactly what Breena did. She closed her eyes, believed in herself, and repeated after her father. "Ek orin di. Do orin di. Snip snap. Fling flung. Up, down, left, right. The ones I've wanted, the ones I've sought. Come to me. Ek orin di. Do orin di."

7

Just like that, Breena could feel herself being lifted off the ground. She couldn't believe her eyes once she saw her reflection; she was looking at her very own wings that were giving off all these wondrous colors. She could finally tell that her wings were different shades of black, blue, and purple, and they were sparkly. She couldn't help herself from feeling like Tinkerbell; now all she needed was her Peter Pan.

Breena still didn't know how to believe in this new reality. All she knew was that she was hearing, seeing, and feeling the impossible; it all felt like a dream.

Aristo Faylinn spoke once again to his daughter. "Breena, hide your wings now, and let me explain some of the responsibilities and rules that come with being a fairy princess.

Number one: Don't let anyone see or touch the *Cryptoria*. So keep it somewhere safe. Remember, the only time you should let someone see the *Cryptoria* is if you trust them. Number two: Be yourself no matter what happens. Remember, no one wants a fake princess; everyone wants a princess who is true. Number three: This one is the

8

most deadly rule. STAY AWAY from silver because it is very deadly to all fairies, pixies, and many other species living in Selectum. Understood?"

"Understood! Papa Bear, can you tell me who these two boys are now?" said the new princess.

Aristo smiled and started explaining. "Of course, they're part of the two families that have been living in our castle for a very long time. These two will be in charge of your safety, because they're your dragon guardians. The tall, tan-skinned one with blue eyes is Warren Nidhogg. The taller, brown-skinned boy with brown eyes is Drake Fafner."

Breena didn't know what to say. She was getting two good-looking dragon guardians, but she didn't understand why they looked like humans.

But before she could ask, Drake spoke. "Princess Faylinn, you're probably wondering why we look like humans instead of being big reptiles with wings. You see, in Selectum all dragons have human forms as well, and we can change into our human form whenever we want. As a matter of fact,

9

most of the time we stay in our human form. The only times we change into our dragon form are when we are about to fly or fight.

We can fight in our human form as well, but our strength is tripled when we're in our dragon forms. Also, if you are wondering, Warren and I don't breathe out fire. Every dragon belongs to one of the four elements, being fire, water, air, and earth. I belong to the air element, and therefore I can breathe out tremendous amount of vicious air. Warren belongs to the water element, and therefore he can breathe out water. Now, if you are ready to say your good-byes to your family, we should get going to Euphoria."

Everything Breena had ever known about reality was turned upside down. She finally understood why her parents were always trying to make her believe in fate, destiny, and the unknown secrets. She decided to say her final byes and have a word with her new friends.

"Wow, I never even knew any of this existed. First things first: it's nice to meet both of you, but please don't call me 'Princess Faylinn.' It sounds too formal and seems more like a label than a name. Since

10

you both are going to be with me all the time, we should be friends. So from now on, you have to call me Breena. And, finally, I guess we should get going, but I just have to go pack. Mom, please help me pack. Dad, what about you guys and Rose?"

Eve couldn't take it any longer; she had to burst out crying and yelling. "Aristo, who told you to be a fairy prince? Because of you my daughter became an elemental fairy and has to go off to some other world away from us, where she's going to have to fight against the evil Joshua. Darling, I'm so sorry that all of this is happening on your birthday. But we can't come there just yet— not until Rose gets her wings. And remember what your grandfather said. He didn't want us coming until the next descendent was on the throne. So until you become queen, we will have to stay here. And your father has already packed your stuff with his magic. Just be safe, and always remember I love you."

Aristo had started tearing up; his firstborn was finally going away from him to fulfill the dreams of their many ancestors. He knew he had to say good-bye to his beautiful angel. "It's all fate. Breena was meant to be the queen of Euphoria. Eve, you know no

11

one can change what's been written in the stars. I love you, honey. Be safe. Boys, show Breena how to get to her palace."

Warren started speaking. "Breena, hold hands with me and Drake. Now close your eyes and start saying, 'Fairyland. Euphoria. Selectum. Kingdom. Castle.'"

Breena just had to do one more thing before they left. She ran toward her parents and gave them a long hug and said, "I love you both so much. Take care. Tell Rose I went to take care of Gramps. Let her know I'm sorry I couldn't wait until she got back home and that I love her very much."

And with that said, she was off holding hands with Warren and Drake. They all started saying, "Fairyland. Euphoria. Selectum. Kingdom. Castle."

Chapter Two:
Euphoria

It felt like only a millisecond had passed since she was saying the mantra with her two friends. But when she opened her eyes, she wasn't standing in her parents' living room but in the most beautiful garden she had ever seen. It had many kinds of flowers growing, a pool, a hot tub, a mermaid fountain, four cars, and two bikes. Some other fairies, pixies, and even two elves were working away. Everything was surrounded with the biggest and fanciest golden fence. But she didn't understand why they had cars when everyone had wings, so she decided to ask Drake and Warren.

"Everything is so beautiful. I just have a question. Why are there cars and bikes parked outside? I mean, I thought every citizen here had wings and could fly places."

13

Warren started laughing and replied, "Well, most of the citizens can fly places. So your grandfather, King Faylinn, announced having hovering vehicles here to help people who can't fly. See, your grandfather wants everyone on Euphoria to act as one. And if you're wondering what I meant when I said most people can fly, then let me explain. You understand that Selectum is a different world than Earth. However, it's a world within Earth—sort of like a parallel dimension—that's connected at the Bermuda Triangle.

"That's why the gravity pull at the Bermuda Triangle outweighs the gravity pull at any other spot on Earth, causing all those myths about disappearances. Well, what happens is that those things and people don't 'disappear.' They simply transport into Selectum, and the entrance happens to be on the border of Euphoria and Felicity. Therefore, sometimes the humans decide to stay over here, but sometimes they want to go back. In order for them to go back, they must get help from one of the citizens of Euphoria or Felicity. If they're lucky, they'll bump into someone nice who's willing to help them and not someone evil who wants to make them into their 'slave.' As a matter of fact, that's how your parents met.

14

"When Princess Eve was researching on the Bermuda Triangle, she ended up coming here and meeting King Joshua, who used to be known as Prince Joshua. You see, his plan was to make her into his slave, but your father saved her. Also, there's a downside of going back to Earth. Once a human goes back to Earth, they remember nothing of Euphoria—"

"Warren, you can tell Breena the rest of this some other time," interrupted Drake. "Let's go inside. She probably wants to meet the king, and I know he wants to meet her."

And just like that, they made their way into the Faylinn Castle.

Once they were inside the castle, Breena could see a ton of little people flying around and cleaning the house. She could also hear a murmuring conversation between a pixie and elf about whether Warren and Drake had succeeded in bringing her. Then she finally heard Drake speak.

"Madam V. We're home."

She wondered who Madam V was until she saw a short, chubby, old fairy flying toward them. Before she knew it, she could hear her speak.

"Hello. Hello. You must be our beautiful princess. My, oh my, you do look just like Eve. But your smile and eyes have come from my little boy, Prince Aristo. I'm Madam V. One of the oldest people working in the castle and the one who raised your father; how is he? I haven't seen him in so long. He sends pictures of all of you, but it's not the same. How are Eve and little Rose doing?"

"Hello. Thank you. They're all doing well. I just wanted to say something. Could everyone just call me Breena? I don't like being called 'princess.' And if you could, would you be kind enough to introduce me to everyone and show me where my Gramps is?" said Breena with a big smile on her face.

Madam V replied, "Of course, my dear. Let us start off with the fairies. There are six of them. These three are ice fairies named Pinky, Daisy, and Rain. While these three are lava fairies named Sunshine, Cloud, and Thunder. Next in line are the seven pixies, all of whom are wind pixies, named Tanya, Ryan, Lisa, Mona, Kevin,

16

Brian, and Sam. And finally we have the five elves. This chubby fellow is Fred; he's the oldest elf in this castle. The rest of them are Mike, Chris, Maria, and Julia, all of whom are fire elves."

"It's nice to meet all of you. Warren, Drake, can you guys take me to my Gramps now?" asked Breena, anxious to see her powerful grandpa.

Drake replied, "Of course, Breena. Do you want to fly to his room? That way you'll be able to use your wings and see our wings."

"OMG. Yes! I want to see your guys' dragon wings," said Breena as she jumped with excitement.

Just like that, she saw her two friends popping out their wings. Breena couldn't believe her eyes. Warren and Drake weren't even in their full dragon forms yet, and they looked so radiant. The wings were so different from hers; their wings were huge. Warren's were tan, filled with red and gold scales, and outlined with a metallic ruby color. Whereas Drake's were brown, filled with blue and bronze scales, and outlined with a darker metallic ruby color.

17

All the sudden she noticed she had shrunk and wondered what had happened. She hadn't shrunk when she was at home.

Warren explained, "You shrunk because you took your full fairy form. If you had just popped out your wings, you would have remained your height."

So Breena fixed her mistake and just popped out her wings and regained her height. And they were off to see her grandfather, the king of Euphoria.

Once they were upstairs, she could see a hallway that was full of rooms. King Faylinn's room was just five feet away from them. Breena realized that she was actually very nervous about meeting her grandpa. She didn't know whether or not she would make a good first impression, but she found the courage and finally entered the room. The first thing she noticed were the purple walls and the really fancy furniture.

She said, "Gramps? I'm here."

King Faylinn turned around, and Breena started to wonder how he could look so sick yet still manage to have a smile

18

on his face. The sight caused tears to start flowing down her cheeks; and before she knew it, she was hugging her grandfather.

When she realized what she was doing, she murmured, "I'm sorry, Gramps. It's just that I can't see you like this."

Her grandfather just smiled and slowly replied, "Welcome to Euphoria. This is going to be your land and your kingdom. My people are your people now. I love you, Breena, and I'm sorry I never came to visit you, but I kept my eye on you and your family. I never wanted your parents to leave. When you were born, I asked your father, Aristo, to name you after your grandmother and come back to live here. But your father was too stubborn to return to Euphoria. I guess he was angry at me for exiling him from his homeland; and because I had said he couldn't step foot into Euphoria until his firstborn sat on the throne. But at least he named you Breena. Don't cry; you're a princess, and princesses don't cry. You have to be strong for me, yourself, your family, your friends, Euphoria, Selectum, even for Earth."

"I understand, Gramps. I love you too. But you have to get better; you can't just pass away like this. I'm going to make sure you follow doctor's orders. I'm a princess; that's fine, but I'm your granddaughter too. And with that right, I'm going to make sure you listen," said Breena

King Faylinn was a little surprised that his sixteen-year-old granddaughter was telling him what to do. But he just started laughing and told Breena that he would listen to everything she said; then explained how Breena needed to rest, because of the long day she was going to face the very next day.

Chapter Three:

SOTA

"WAKE UP! WAKE UP! WAKE UP! You have school, sleepyhead. It's already six a.m., and the boys are almost ready. Hurry up and go take a shower. Your school starts at nine a.m. Breakfast is already made," said Madam V.

After trying on approximately nine outfits, she chose to wear blue jeans, a black tank top, and a red varsity jacket. Then decided to practice using her wings by flying down the stairs, where she could see a table filled with food; and her two foolish friends pretending to have a sword fight with butter knives. Breena could also see her grandfather there waiting for her to go to school.

"Well, well, look at the sleepyhead finally coming down for her first day at SOTA," joked Drake as Breena started eating her breakfast.

21

As soon as she finished, she said, "Let's get going to school. How far is it from here anyways?"

Warren then reminded her of the easy way of travelling in Euphoria. So the three friends stood in a circle, held hands, closed their eyes, and started saying the mantra, "Fairyland. Euphoria. Selectum. Spirits of the Air."

When they opened their eyes, they were standing on the campus of Breena's new school, Sprits of the Air. Breena thought to herself about how this school's campus was probably one of the nicest campuses she had ever seen. There were multiple parking lots, a very big field where some students were playing some kind of game, green trees and bushes, and benches with some students studying; the school's building was just as beautiful as the campus.

It was a big building or maybe many buildings put together to give the illusion of being one. Either way, it was gorgeously lined with many doors, windows, and long pathways. Breena was happy that her new school looked like a fun place to be—at least from the outside it looked like a fun place. She wasn't sure how the teachers would be.

22

"Breena let me introduce you to my girlfriend. This is Nixie, the pixie," said Drake as he stood beside a girl with pointy ears, hazel eyes, black hair with purple streaks, and wearing a short white dress with strapped flats.

"Hellooooooo. It's very nice to meet you. How are you doing, Breena? How do you like Euphoria, Selectum? Is it very different from Earth? Oh, sorry, Warren. I didn't even notice you. Are you going to be taking part in the dragon fight today?" said Nixie.

Breena was surprised at how fast Drake's girlfriend was talking, but she still answered her. "It's very nice to meet you as well. I'm getting used to all the changes. And, yes, it's different and yet similar to Earth. Warren, what's a dragon fight?"

"NIXIE! I *TOLD* YOU NOT TO TALK ABOUT THOSE! Breena, please don't let anyone know that I take part in dragon fights. They're sort of frowned upon, so I can get into a lot of trouble. They're fights that dragons of any kind take part in to gain strength and experience of fighting. Then they can use it for when they need to fight in the field—for example, in the upcoming war. But let's get heading inside,

23

because our first class is something that will help you out a lot in the future, 'Euphorian History.' and our teacher can be a pain; he hates when people are late, so let's go," answered Warren.

As they entered the school, Breena started noticing a lot of similarities between SOTA and her old school. For example, they were both filled with lockers and cliques.

"I guess all schools are the same, whether on Earth or on Selectum. But this is my new school, my new friends, my new life," thought Breena.

But as they were getting closer to the classroom, she couldn't help but feel frightened about everything. Nixie and Drake had already entered the classroom, but Breena asked them to save seats for Warren and herself.

Then she turned to Warren and started speaking. "Warren, could you please finish your story? You know the one about my mom, dad, and that Joshua person?"

"You're really interested in knowing, eh? Okay, well, how about this: let's head

24

to class right now. I mean Mr. Simpson is a nice teacher, but he's very strict. Therefore, I'll explain everything to you after school. When Drake will be gone to water ball tryouts with Nixie. I'll take you to my secret spot that no one knows about and tell you there, alright?" smirked Warren.

Breena opened the classroom door and said, "Sounds good." Then she noticed that everyone in the class was staring at her exactly like a little child looking into a candy shop. "I'm sorry, Mr. Simpson. I didn't know that you had started taking attendance already. It's my fault that we're late. I couldn't find the right book, so I asked Warren to help me out because I didn't want to be unprepared for my first day," explained Breena.

Mr. Simpson just laughed and said, "I guess you're our new princess, Miss Breena Faylinn? It's quite alright; I'll let it go today because it's your first day. However, next time please try to get here before I start taking attendance."

"Yo, Mr. Simpson! Sorry about being late. What's this? Is the new princess already planning on stealing my long-standing status of being the late student?" said a mysterious male from behind Breena.

25

There was something familiar about that voice; she had heard it before. But she couldn't remember where. When she turned around to see who it was, she couldn't recognize who he was and yet felt some kind of attraction to him. There was something about the way he looked at her; had she seen or spoken to him somewhere? Who was he?

"Welcome to class, Mr. Vritra. This is your absolute last warning. Now, all three of you—Ms. Faylinn, Mr. Nidhogg, and Mr. Vritra—get to your seats," said the now annoyed Mr. Simpson.

Breena, Warner, and the mysterious guy all started taking their seats. Breena went and sat beside Nixie, and Warner sat across from her, beside Drake. And the mysterious guy who seemed like the renegade of the classroom went to sit in a desk that was placed at the back of the class, isolated from everyone else.

Breena couldn't stop herself from turning and looking at this mysterious guy. She began noticing little things about him. He was wearing a white shirt, black leather jacket, tight black jeans, and black shoes. His skin was light brown, his hair was blackish brown, and his eyes were either light brown

26

or hazel; she couldn't tell because of the distance between the two of them.

He looked up and saw her looking at him; Breena looked away feeling a bit awkward about their eyes meeting.

Nevertheless, he just smirked and spoke. "Mr. S, let's start learning something useful because our future queen needs to learn our Euphorian history as soon as possible—especially if she wants to step up to run our wonderful Euphoria properly."

She saw Warren getting irritated as he started speaking. "Maybe if you shut up, Mr. S will start his lesson. Plus, Breena already has leadership skills running through her blood. She doesn't need any 'lessons' on how to 'step up' to lead a country to prosperity."

"Oh, wow, Warren. You sure are sticking up for our new princess quite nicely. Why is that? What? Are you already falling for her? Well, my naive little cousin, we shall see how things go when she has to face the upcoming war. Let's just hope she doesn't end up running back to Earth." argued the mystery man, who was apparently cousins with Warren.

27

Breena looked at Warren, who was very angry; his eyes had even started to change colors. It seemed as if he was about to take on his full dragon form.

However, he just raised his voice and yelled back at his cousin in the most vicious voice, "WATCH WHAT YOU SAY BLAZE! Let's not start a fight here! She's our future queen! I suggest you learn some damn respect if you know what's good for you."

And just like that, Blaze stood up to fight.

"BOYS! Sit down! If you want to fight, do it on the streets! Don't you dare fight in *my* classroom! DO YOU UNDERSTAND THAT, VRITRA and NIDHOGG?" yelled Mr. Simpson.

"That was unexpected. Just stay calm, Warren. You know Blaze is just being himself; don't let him bother you," said Drake.

Nixie, feeling the awkward situation in the group, said, "Breena, would you like to work with us on the assignment? Both of us can do research with the textbooks,

28

and the boys can use the computers to find information; I think this assignment will help you learn your heritage."

"Huh? Um, yeah, sure. Let's do it up. Warren, what's wrong? Why do you look so irritated? Listen to Drake, and don't let anything bother you; just ignore it," said Breena.

"Drake, you heard Nixie. Let's go to the computers and get our part of the information," announced Warren as he started walking away without answering Breena's question.

Chapter Four:
Blaze Vritra

⊙⊙

"Nixie, what's wrong with Warren? Is he angry with me? Oh, wait, what's the assignment on?" asked Breena.

Nixie didn't know how to answer, but she decided to give it a try. "Um, well, first things first: our assignment is to find information on the two royal families that founded Euphoria. Second, to be honest I'm not sure if Warren is angry or worried. I'll try my best to explain. That guy you keep looking at; his name is Blaze Vritra, and he belongs to the second founding family. In other words, he's the descendant of the second royal family of Euphoria. He's a fire-breathing pixrie dragon, the second of his kind, and cousins with Warren from his dad's side. But Warren dislikes him for some reason; so maybe he's just worried about you getting hurt by Blaze."

30

Breena wasn't sure how to react but she had questions. And since it seemed like Nixie was the only one willing to give her information, she asked her, "What's a fire-breathing pixrie dragon? If he's part of a royal family, does that mean we're related? And if he has family drama with Warren, does that mean I can't be friends with Blaze?"

"His mom was a half fairy and half pixie, therefore making him a pixrie. His father on the other hand was a fire-breathing guardian dragon. Actually, if I'm not wrong, his father was one of your fathers' best friends, and he used to work for your grandfather. But I'm not sure on all the details. Anyways, since Blaze's father was a fire-breathing guardian dragon and his mom was a pixrie, he became the strongest and the most magical being on Selectum. Everyone is scared of him because no one else has his kind of power. Also, so far no one has been able to hurt him or even affect him in any way. As rumor has it, you might have equal strength and magic as him. Another thing, no one can stop you from becoming friends with him; you shouldn't worry about the family drama between him and Warren.

"I mean, Blaze is a nice guy. I know that for a fact because I used to be good

31

friends with him. But after I started dating Drake, I drifted away from him. Breena, I can tell that you sort of like him already, so let me tell you that you're not related by blood in any form. All I'm going to say is, you shouldn't worry; just follow your heart," explained Nixie.

Breena didn't know how to react; she felt a strong attraction and some kind of connection with a guy that one of her good friends hated. Suddenly, Breena started hearing a voice in her head. It was the same voice she had heard calling out her name when she woke up on her birthday—the voice she had fallen in love with. But this time he sounded cruel.

Breena listened closely to what he was saying. "Well, well, Princess Breena. You should really watch your back. You don't even know anything about your heritage, your kingdom or even yourself. If you want to make sure you learn proper magic in time for the war, I would suggest you stop fooling yourself and study up. Also, keep the *Cryptoria* safe; I know you have it. And maybe—just maybe—if you study it, you'll learn something of value."

32

Breena wasn't sure whose voice it was, but she had a good idea. She turned around to look at Blaze and just thought to herself, "Don't tell me what to do! I suggest you get out of *my head*! I knew your voice sounded familiar!"

Without even realizing it, she had put Blaze on his knees, trembling in what looked like pain.

When she turned around to face her partner, she saw a terrified Nixie and whispered, "What did I just do? Oh, God, do you think anyone noticed what happened?"

Except before Nixie could answer, they saw the two boys coming back with their part of the assignment done. And just like that, class was finished.

As the day progressed, Breena couldn't stop thinking about how she had put Blaze in pain and how both of them could hear one another.

It was the beginning of lunch, and Blaze's voice had re-entered her mind. "Can you please come to the field by the bleachers?

33

But don't tell anyone, because I don't want to start a fight again."

So Breena waited for her three friends and told them she had to go to the washroom. Yet instead she headed to the field to meet Prince Blaze Vritra.

"Okay, I'm here. What in the universe do you want now? Did you want to insult me some more? Or did you want to ask me if 'Earth' girls just go around fooling around with their friends, like you asked Warren in front of our first period class? Really, for a prince I thought you would have a little bit more respect and manners, but apparently not.

"We had three classes together so far, and you didn't even bother talking to me, so why now? Why would you call me all the way to the damn bleachers to talk? Oh, and by the way, you should really start talking instead of standing there, staring at me like some kind of lost dragon pixrie boy. Seriously! Tell me what you want!" yelled Breena.

"Have you been doing research on me or something? How do you know that I'm a pixrie dragon who happens to be a prince? Well, I just wanted to apologize for the things I said in first period. I shouldn't have spoken that way; I guess it's not your fault that you didn't get to grow up in Euphoria. I just hope you find it in your heart to forgive me. I asked you not to bring or tell your friends because Warren and Drake hate me due to some events from our past. And Nixie used to be my best friend, but she deserted me when she started dating Drake.

I just don't trust any of them. And since you're a royal member, I thought I should warn you not to trust anyone, particularly because you have the *Cryptoria*; please keep it safe. The priest trusted your family with it, and I know that you won't break his trust. But the real reason to why I called you here is that I actually wanted to know, how you managed to cause me pain? And how we could hear one another without even moving our lips? Have you been able to do that with anyone else? Because I'll be honest, I've tried to send telepathic messages to many people, but I haven't been able to," explained Blaze.

Breena didn't understand what had just occurred. Was this the same Blaze that everyone hated? It couldn't have been him, because this person was trying to look out for her well-being. He was the one seeming

35

so alone; and the one person who sounded like he actually cared about her. Not to mention, that they were both looking for the answers to the same questions.

How could they connect so well? Was it because they were both part of royal Euphorian families? Or was it because of something else? Breena couldn't help but feel sort of sorry for him.

After what seemed like a very long time of silence, Blaze spoke again. "Is it possible for us to try to send telepathic messages to one another right now? I mean, if you don't mind."

"Why would you want to do that? What are you trying to prove? I don't know all my magic tricks right now. But seriously, this is just annoying. You first insult me, then show me your soft side, and now ask me for this telepathic message. What are you up to?" messaged Breena to Blaze, only to get a reply that she didn't even expect.

"I was just wondering if you could re-enter my mind. Because for some reason you're the only person I can send telepathic messages to, and it seems like I'm

36

the only person you can send telepathic messages to. But you can control my actions as well.

I think that's something I'm not even capable of; that's your special power. I understand that you don't know that much magic yet, but if you want, I can maybe try teaching you some royal magic before the war. Because, believe it or not, I want you to be prepared for the war; Felicity will do anything—and I mean anything—to get the *Cryptoria* from you.

If you can block them out and learn defensive and offensive magic, you'll be prepared for the war. But for that, you need to learn royal magic, which is the most advanced magic in Euphoria. But to learn it, two members of the royal families are needed: one member from each family. So that's why I'm saying both of us can maybe train together. Plus, I know more about Euphorian history, at least more than your precious guardian dragons, more than Nixie, and definitely more than you.

Anyways, enough of this. You should get back to your friends. But if you ever need my help or want me to help you learn anything about your heritage or magic, just give me a telepathic message. Oh, and, Breena, Happy Belated Birthday. I don't know if you got my telepathic message yesterday morning when I tried talking to you. I didn't get a reply, so I'm not sure."

"I heard you when you spoke to me on my birthday. That's why I recognized your voice. Would you help me learn my family history and some royal magic?" messaged Breena as she walked into the school to find her three friends finishing up their lunch.

She got a simple telepathic reply from Blaze. "Whenever you want to learn, just let me know."

Chapter Five:
Aristo & Eve

The whole afternoon Breena couldn't stop thinking about the conversation she had with Blaze. But she was looking forward to learning the rest of the information about her parents from Warren. After what seemed like forever, her classes had finished. Drake and Nixie were gone for water ball tryouts, and Warren had finally showed up.

"Let's go. We're flying," he said.

Slowly they were up high, flying through the clouds, going over trees and buildings.

After a while Breena looked down and saw her castle. However, a few minutes later, she saw another castle.

"That's Blaze's castle, just in case you're wondering. The place I'm taking you

39

is right there, so start slowing down your wings," explained Warren.

They were on the ground now, standing in front of a small cottage with a sign that read, **THE NIDHOGGS**.

"This is my family cottage. But since my family moved into your castle, no one ever comes here anymore. But at the end of the day, this is my home, so I come here once in a while. Let's go inside and talk about what you want to know," said Warren.

"Okay, well, I guess first I want to know how my mom still remembers everything about Euphoria when you said when a human returns to Earth, they forget everything. Secondly, please finish telling me about my parents and Joshua. I just need to understand how my parents met and why Gramps kicked my parents out to live on Earth. I mean, my dad told me how Gramps had asked him to marry someone else. But still, totally kicking them out? Isn't that a bit extreme?" asked Breena.

Warren thought for a moment and then started speaking. "Well, like I said yesterday, your mother, Eve, lived on Earth and went to conduct research on the Bermuda

40

Triangle; that was when she got transported into Selectum because of the gravity pull; and was found by Felicity's present king, who happens to be Joshua, a very evil man.

But your father, Prince Aristo, was playing water ball at the moment, which is sort of similar to the Earth game called handball. Anyways back to the main story: your father heard your mother screaming, fought with Joshua, saved your mother, and brought her back to your castle.

When your grandfather found out, he was very happy that your father saved someone from becoming a slave and brought her to the castle for safety. With time King Faylinn became very attached to Eve, to the point where he treated her like a daughter. And at the same time, your father had started falling in love with her.

Whereas, your grandfather had given his word to Blaze's grandparents that Prince Aristo would marry their daughter. In other words, King Faylinn wanted Prince Faylinn to marry Blaze's mother, Princess Shaylee Eolande. But she was in love with your father's best friend, Andrew Vritra, my uncle. Well, when your father tried explaining his position to his father, it went horribly

41

wrong. Your grandfather banned Prince Aristo from Euphoria and told him to go live on Earth with Princess Eve. He said that he would never have the privilege of sitting on the throne, and he wouldn't be allowed to step foot into Euphoria until his first-born took up the title of being either king or queen; unless circumstances allowed him to come back. As for Uncle Andrew, he got kicked out from the castle and was married to Princess Shaylee.

Your mother still remembers everything because she's married to the prince of Euphoria; therefore, she's a member of the royal family. Also, once a human has a child with a citizen of Euphoria and returns to Earth, that person always has a memory of everything that took place on Euphoria. It's just like when the citizens of Euphoria go to Earth to visit. Once a person is a citizen, they can come and go as they please; no restrictions. But that's about it. Do you have any other questions?"

Breena thought for a second and then started speaking. "Actually, I do have one more question. If you don't mind me asking, could you tell me why you don't get along with your cousin Blaze?"

42

Warren looked down with a frown and answered. "The thing is, as children, we were very close; I used to always hang out at his house, and his father was my favorite uncle. But my father didn't like Uncle Andrew because of his so-called betrayal with your family.

However, when we were six or seven years old, my father decided to take me and Drake to the border by the river to play water ball, and Blaze was there with his father. Finally, after so many years, our fathers were talking and having fun together; we thought our families were going to become close again. But just then King Joshua tried to attack Euphoria. Therefore, Uncle Andrew made us hide behind a bush and covered us with a magical shield. Then our fathers fought against Joshua and his men. Joshua ended up shooting a silver arrow toward Blaze's father, and my father saved him but got killed because of that one arrow to his heart.

"I was crying so much and wanted to go to him, but Blaze didn't let us get out of the shield. Then another arrow was shot, and this time it hit Uncle Andrew. The Felicity citizens walked away laughing; I guess they assumed they had killed everyone. So we

43

waited until they were out of sight, and then we ran to our fathers. I lost my father because of Blaze's dad, and Blaze didn't let me go to him before he passed away. I didn't get to say good-bye to him; that's why I can't stand Blaze. Every time I see him, all I think about is my father's dead body. Anyways, we should probably get back home before King Faylinn starts to worry about you."

The two friends didn't talk the whole fly home. Breena was saddened and shocked about the recent news she had heard. Everything she had ever thought about her parents was a lie. Her parents had an amazing love story. Her grandfather had kicked his own son out of the country to another world just because his son wanted to marry the girl of his choice, and Blaze's mother had almost been her father's wife. However, Breena was glad that her father didn't marry Blaze's mother. If those two had married, she wouldn't have been born or been able to encounter Blaze Vritra. Not to mention, the information between Warren's and Blaze's families was just horrible. **Dear Diary:**

Everything has changed since my last entry. I'm no longer on Earth but instead in a parallel world called Selectum and in a country named Euphoria. That's not all I found

44

out. I'm actually an elemental fairy princess, not some human girl like I always thought. I also learned that I have to start studying everything about my heritage because of an upcoming war. I don't know how I'm handling all of this. I miss my parents and sister so much right now, but I guess I can't do anything about it.

Although, right now I'm thinking that my mother was right—you know, about her "fate" nonsense. I'm saying that because today my friend told me about how my parents met. To be honest after hearing their story; it seems like somehow they were meant to meet one another so then I would be born. I believe I was destined to meet Blaze Vritra. He's the boy whose voice I heard calling out to me yesterday morning! I know it sounds bizarre, but it really does feel as if we're meant to be together. However, I think he tries to make people think that he's a jerk, because I know that he has a kind soul.

Maybe he's trying to make people hate him so no one leaves him. I found out a lot of saddening information about his past; it honestly broke my heart. His best friend Nixie stopped being friends with him because she started dating my friend Drake. Also, his

45

cousin Warren hates his guts because of the way their fathers passed away. I don't think he deserves to be treated like that; I mean, he deserves the respect and love that I'm getting. After all, he's a member of the second royal family and, therefore, a prince.

Another thing: I didn't have that dream last night. The first time in many years I didn't see any guy or even a duplicate girl; it's as if, since I came here, my dreams have vanished. Maybe I'll never know why I saw that boy and that Mimi girl. Wouldn't it be funny if that guy ended up being Blaze in some way? Anyways, I have to go to sleep. I just hope that in the future I'm destined to have a beautiful love story like my parents, Eve and Aristo, did.

Sincerely,

Breena Faylinn

Chapter Six:
The Royal Prophecy

Two weeks had nearly gone by since Breena had started attending SOTA. During this time she became very close friends with Nixie, Drake, and Warren, but her eyes kept longing to see Blaze. Breena didn't understand what to do; she hadn't even gotten any telepathic messages from him.

Another week had slowly passed, and she couldn't take it anymore; therefore, she decided to telepathically speak to him. "*Blaze*! Where are you? I need to start practicing the royal magic. So please, help me."

An additional three days had vanished into thin air, but there was no reply from Blaze. However, just as Breena was about to give up on hearing back from him, she heard his voice. "I'm at the border with three other people, making sure no one enters Euphoria. Didn't your friends tell you anything? The news about King Faylinn has gotten out. So now Felicity citizens know he's very sick, and some of their people have started sneaking in; but now I think they've stopped. Don't worry, I'll take care of them, but you concentrate on keeping the *Cryptoria* safe. I think tonight it'll be harmless if I come back for a couple of hours. I'll pick you up at six thirty p.m. be ready, Princess; it'll be our first date."

Breena was frightened Felicity had already started sneaking in, and Blaze was one of the four people keeping them out. Why hadn't her friends told her anything or even gone to help Blaze and the others? But the prince was right; she didn't need to be troubled about that. He would take care of it, and she needed to make sure the *Cryptoria* was out of any possible danger. Plus, she had bigger worries.

How would she tell her Grandfather about her date? Would she be allowed to even go? And the biggest thing: what would she wear? It was already four thirty p.m., meaning Breena only had two hours. She kept thinking of ways to tell her grandfather and then finally got the courage to ask.

"Gramps, can I come into your room? I need to talk to you about something very important. I have agreed to go on a date with Prince Vritra."

"Come in, my dear. Did you say Prince Vritra? You mean young Blaze? If so, you should be getting ready. Don't worry, I'll make sure Warren and Drake leave you guys alone when you're on your date," answered King Faylinn.

Breena didn't know how to respond; her grandfather didn't even question her about her decision. Instead he seemed to be happy with her choice. Therefore, she decided not to worry about it. While getting ready, she hummed songs and thought about how her date would go. But she hadn't even noticed the time. It was already Six p.m., and just then she heard a knock on her bedroom window.

It was Blaze. "Wow. You really do make a beautiful princess. Come downstairs. I came early to talk with your grandfather."

49

Breena couldn't believe it; their first date was really going to happen. When she arrived downstairs, she saw Blaze, Warren, Nixie, Drake, and her Gramps sitting down and talking. It seemed like Blaze was explaining something serious to her grandfather.

"How are you doing, Your Majesty? I'm assuming that you've heard about those nasty Felicity people trying to sneak into our territory during the past few weeks. We fought off most of them; some were killed, and some flew back. However, I think everyone should be on the watch because some of them might have snuck in. I have warned Breena to keep the *Cryptoria* safe. She will be a target now since everyone knows that she's new to Euphoria, Selectum. That is why I have decided to help Breena learn more about her heritage, more about the information in the *Cryptoria*. And I'm confident that we will be able to practice the royal magic."

"I have full faith in you, Blaze. Just make sure that all of you on the border are safe. Warren and Drake, tonight you guys will keep away from Breena; and will go to the border for six hours every day between six thirty p.m. and twelve thirty a.m. In these six hours, Blaze, you'll be training

50

Breena. This means that today you have six hours to be with her, but she must be home at twelve thirty a.m. Another thing: since you brought up the royal magic, I should warn you that no one has been able to do it since it was invented by our ancestors; so all I can say is good luck. Oh, and, Nixie, I want you to go and tell the citizens to be safe and report anyone out of the ordinary."

Breena was surprised that everyone was actually being a team for once. "I guess this is how political families and people work in general. When they need one another, they'll work together," she said to Blaze as they started to walk outside of the castle.

She still couldn't believe that she was going on her first date with him. The best part was that her Gramps had given permission to them. But now, Breena had started feeling nervous. The only other date she had ever been on was a lunch date with her best friend's brother.

As they finally reached outside, Breena saw Blaze's red and black motorcycle, which made her even more worried. And the awkward silence wasn't helping the situation.

51

Therefore, she decided to talk. "You look very handsome, and I like your dragon buckle; it really represents you."

"Thank you. My father gave me this buckle right before he passed away. Hold on tight. I don't want you falling off my motorcycle once it starts flying. I'm taking you to the Royal Garden; as legend goes, it's the most beautiful place in Euphoria. Apparently when Euphoria was founded by our families, the priest that was with them chose the ruling family and made a royal prophecy. The prophecy said, 'Only members of the two royal families can enter this garden. But the light that will lead everyone to victory will shine when the two that are meant to be one will come together. Only then will the two royal families learn to rule as a single power.' No one really knows what that means. I'll explain more about the prophecy when we get inside; it's written down on a tomb in the garden. Anyways' Breena, I need you to repeat a mantra after me, because without the mantra the gate won't open," explained Blaze.

She was so interested in hearing his voice that she didn't even notice how quickly they had reached the garden. But that didn't matter to her; all that she cared about was

52

that they were there together, and it was time to open the gate.

They both started stating the mantra. "Open yourself to the prince and princess of Euphoria. Prince Blaze Vritra and Princess Breena Faylinn are here seeking entrance to the garden. Oh, great spirits of our ancestors, allow us to come in and learn the royal magic and to be blessed by the spirit of our royal priest."

With that, the gate had opened, and Breena couldn't believe her eyes. Blaze was right. This was the most gorgeous place in Euphoria.

The flowers, trees, river, and the waterfall were all arranged to look like a giant bird's face and body. Tombs were lined up in the middle, and one of them must have had the story of the prophecy written on it. This was it; she was going to learn how to use royal magic and start learning about their heritage. Breena and Blaze started going toward the tomb, but something was changing; it was Blaze.

He was holding her hand as he murmured into her ear, "You have to say, 'Princess Breena Faylinn, member of the first royal family' after I say, 'Prince Blaze Vritra, member of the second Royal family.' And then we both have to say, 'We are here to learn the prophecy and the royal magic. Bless us to learn what is needed to keep the *Cryptoria* and Euphoria safe.'"

Breena could sense the nervousness in Blaze's voice but still knew that she could rely on him to train her. She couldn't explain it to anyone, but Blaze was one of the only people that she could blindly trust; Breena didn't know if that was because of the connection they shared or because of something else. But she did as he said, and in the matter of a couple seconds, words creating a story appeared on the tomb, that belonged to the royal priest himself.

Magus Skelly

Royal Priest

01/10/1389–03/13/1485

"Blaze Vritra and Breena Faylinn, you have asked to see the royal prophecy from many years ago and to learn the royal magic. Well then, this is the royal prophecy: There will come a time in the future when a great war will be on the doorstep of Euphoria. The two royal families will be united as one. Against all the odds they will learn to work together and run the country as a single power.

The two that have been chosen by destiny will share a connection that won't be seen by anyone else. They will share the same strengths, weaknesses, and skills that Princess Mimi Faylinn and Prince Thomas 'Tommy' Eolande once did. Some might say they will be the reincarnation of these two lovers who couldn't make it alive to the ceremony of 'Creating Euphoria.' However, the chosen two will be one soul split into two bodies, two hearts with a single rhythmic feeling, and one mind shared by two brains; they will make one another whole. The royal light leading to freedom and prosperity will shine when these two realize they're destined to be together.

To learn the royal magic, you must clear your minds and become one with nature. You must accept who you are, accept your element, and believe in yourself; because as everyone knows, if you lack self-confidence, you lack the skill to rule. You must learn how to work with your surroundings. If you want to know defensive magic, you must learn how to protect yourself from nature. And if you want to study offensive magic, you must learn how to attack using your elements. Above all, you must remember to never let your country down and to become familiar with your strengths and weaknesses."

Chapter Seven:
Blaze & Breena

The writing on the tomb had slowly vanished, leaving Breena stunned; as she decided to start talking. "Blaze, the prophecy said, 'Mimi Faylinn.' I need to tell you something really serious, something that I haven't told anyone else, except my diary, of course. You see, when I was on Earth, I used to have dreams—well, I guess visions—of this blurry boy. And then the night before my sixteenth birthday, I saw him clearly from behind, and he was looking up at a girl dressed in a beautiful gown; she looked like a princess. Then he said her name, 'Mimi.' Do you think it's possible that it was the same girl? Did I see my ancestor in my dream? I don't know how to explain it, but the Mimi I saw looked exactly like me. Coincidently this all happened before I heard your voice for the first time and before I learned about Euphoria."

Blaze was astonished. He didn't know what to say, but he knew Breena was waiting for a reply. "Are you sure you saw Princess Mimi Faylinn? Don't get me wrong, but it's just that the dream you explained sounds similar to the images I used to have before you came to Euphoria. I used to see a girl, but her face was always blurry. Then the night before your sixteenth birthday, I dreamed I was in a castle. I could see a female looking downstairs at some guy in a black tuxedo who looked exactly like me. Then she replied to him, saying, 'Thomas you need to be patient for your dance.'

"Is it possible that we were having the same dream? About some kind of meeting between these two? Do you think we're connected with them? Also, when I woke up, somehow my brain automatically said, 'Happy sixteenth birthday, Princess. I've been waiting for you, but be careful this time; we don't want something going wrong.' When I realized what I was saying, I thought I was still thinking about my dream and maybe trying to speak with that girl. I didn't know that my message had actually gone through telepathically to you, until the next day when I saw you in class and succeeded in sending you the telepathic message."

58

Breena wasn't sure how to answer Blaze. She was more nervous than she had ever been; her dream might have been some kind of reality. But why was she having the same dreams that Blaze used to have? She didn't know how to react; all she knew was that she wanted to prepare herself for the war.

She said, "Perhaps we can talk about them in a while, but first I need you to help me learn what element I belong to. Otherwise I won't be able to do the royal magic."

Blaze understood and started explaining what she had to do. "I need you to close your eyes, clear your mind, and do as the tomb said: become familiar with your surroundings because only then you will know what your element is. You should feel yourself becoming one with a certain element. For example, if you get attracted to the river, you'll be water."

Breena did exactly as he said, and slowly she started feeling the air fighting the leaves. She could sense the heat as hot as pure fire coming down from the sun as it lightly burned the little insects on the trees. She could even feel the waves being made by the waterfall clashing with the riverbank. How

59

was this possible? She was being attracted to all the elements. What did that mean? She opened her eyes and saw a smile on Blaze's face.

She gently explained what had happened when she was becoming one with nature. "I can feel everything: the air, the fire, and the water. It's as if all the elements are working together with me."

"That means my thought was right. There is no other explanation for why you could control my actions. You have the rarest element; you have Earth. But it does make a lot of sense because of three things. Number one: You're an elemental fairy, meaning you technically contain the skills to control all the elements. And just so you know, you happen to be the only elemental fairy of our time. Number two: You have the kind soul that has the strength to handle all the elements. Number three: You grew up on Earth; therefore it makes sense that you'd have the earth element.

Anyways, the earth element enables a creature to control the actions of others. It's a great defensive and offensive skill, but you need to learn how to use this element

60

for your benefit," explained Blaze as he held Breena in a tight embrace.

He had just begun noticing the little details about her. His nose could sense her smell of lavender with a hint of vanilla, and his heart could feel the simplicity that made up her beautiful soul. However, there was something else that attracted him to her. It was the way her big brown eyes lit up when she looked at him; it was her smile that made everything feel right.

Blaze didn't know what was happening to him. He had never felt this way about anyone before; his heartbeats had started becoming one with Breena's. And before he knew what was going on, he started pulling Breena even closer to himself.

As they both closed their eyes and interlocked their lips for a tender kiss. Their first kiss; it was perfect. When the two of them opened their eyes, they couldn't believe what they were seeing. It had started raining in the garden, and a bright light was surrounding the two of them.

Breena looked up and saw that Blaze had opened up his dragon wings. They were the most exquisite wings she had ever seen.

They were fairly large and were colored dark blue and light brown, and were outlined with a metallic gold color. However, his right wing had a single crown-shaped red scale, and he had a large scar on the bottom of his left wing. And at that moment Breena noticed how much taller Blaze was than her and how she felt safe with his muscular arms wrapped around her.

"The light shining around us—it has to be the same radiant light the prophecy was speaking about. We're the chosen couple, the chosen royals that will lead everyone to freedom and prosperity. I mean, think about it: 'A war will be on the doorstep of Euphoria.' We came here to train for the war. The priest's tomb spoke about a connection no one else would see; we can telepathically speak to one another and not anyone else. When our lips met for that marvelous kiss, our hearts, our souls, our minds, and all of our surroundings figured out that we are destined to be one. Our souls have been joined together by the gods. And it's not only in this lifetime but from when I was Mimi Faylinn and you were Thomas 'Tommy' Eolande.

"That's why we kept having the same dream as one another over and over again;

we thought they were random images when in reality they were memories from our past life. Now together we must prepare ourselves to lead our Euphoria to prosperity and keep all the citizens safe," Breena said as she jumped up with joy.

Everything made perfect sense now. It was the reason she had fallen in love with Blaze's voice when she first heard it on her birthday. It explained that instant attraction when she first saw him in Mr. Simpson's class. Her mother was right. Everything about her life was written in the stars from way before she was born; it was all destiny.

Blaze thought about it for a while, and then, with a grin on his face, he started speaking. "I guess you're right. We must be the chosen two, otherwise we wouldn't have so many similarities to the people described in the prophecy, and the light wouldn't have started shining around us. But that means we have to fulfill the responsibility given to us, and, therefore, we have to start training right away. However, maybe we should learn more about Mimi Faylinn and Thomas 'Tommy' Eolande. I mean, since they—or, I guess, us—since we created the royal magic, it should be easy for us to learn it. Don't you think? Now, Breena, feel free to disagree, but if you trust me enough, we should perhaps take a look in the *Cryptoria* to learn more about their story, about who they were, and about how they passed away."

Chapter Eight:
Tommy & Mimi

Breena agreed with Blaze and decided to look for the graves of the two former lovers. Once they had found the graves of the princess and prince, they opened the *Cryptoria* to start reading their history.

"This is the love story of our beloved Princess and Prince. For starters, you should know that Princess Mimi Faylinn was a human fairy, a person we stated as an elemental fairy, and Prince Thomas 'Tommy' Eolande was a dragon pixrie. They were the first hybrid creatures in the history of Selectum, and their powers were unlike any other; they were best friends from the very start. As these two turned twelve years old, they started practicing a new kind of magic that no one else could do. They named it the royal magic.

65

Almost all of Princess Mimi's magic was made up by combining the elements together; no one knows how she was able to do it. Prince Eolande used to say, 'she belongs to the Earth element, which is only possible by a person: who has a kind soul and has some type of connection to Earth. By definition, it can be done by a human fairy, because humans adapt to any kind of element.' That's the only proper clarification anyone has ever given about the Earth element.

Everything was going well until that day: the day of Princess Faylinn's sixteenth birthday. Prince Eolande's' distinct cousin came into our then present country named Felicity and tried to flirt with our precious Princess."

"Wait a minute, Blaze. It says, 'Our then present country named Felicity.' That means before our families founded Euphoria, we lived and ruled over Felicity. It also says, 'her sixteenth birthday.' Perhaps that's why we kept having that dream. I mean, it would make sense since we saw a clear image the night before my sixteenth birthday. Something went wrong on that day. That's why our souls were showing us that specific scene," said Breena, as they continued reading.

66

"Our Prince couldn't handle what he was seeing; he knew that his cousin, Prince James, was a horrible man. But he never knew James was so horrible that he would start flirting with our Prince's' girlfriend. But that wasn't the end of his cousin's' hideous acts. As soon as the prince started a fight to protect his soul mate and future wife, his cousin and uncles showed their true forms. They decided to take over Felicity, kill the prince and princess, and steal the tricks of doing the royal magic created by Mimi and Tommy's true love.

The day after the princess's sixteenth birthday, Prince James and his people started attacking the unprepared royals. However, Princess Mimi and Prince Tommy both showed their powers on that day. They fought with all their might and convinced their families and me, Priest Magus Skelly, to exit Felicity and enter the land that was named Euphoria. That was a special birthday present for Princess Mimi given by the prince himself. We didn't want to abandon them there, but they forced us to leave them alone and let them fight.

"To keep us safe on our journey, our Princess used a special defensive skill she had created, and they used their offensive

67

skills to fight. Furthermore, our Princess and Prince, not caring about themselves, tried their best to keep the *Cryptolicity* safe. But those cruel and dimwitted people under James's leadership didn't have any mercy on our children; they got out a large silver arrow and shot at our Prince and Princess."

"Stop reading," said Blaze as his eyes started becoming watery by remembering the horrible event that had taken place. "I think I remember what happened. My cousin from back then, Prince James, started shooting silver arrows at us, but we fought them like crazy. However, when he took out the large arrow, it wasn't shot at us but at the *Cryptolicity*. Then with his magic, he turned the front of the arrow into a large hand and stole the *Cryptolicity*. He knew that we couldn't touch silver, otherwise we would've died. But we kept fighting with them and ended up killing most of their men; then we made our way across the border into Euphoria."

Breena was ready to learn the power from her past life; she had somehow started remembering how to do all of her magical powers. "Blaze, I know. I remember everything too. We made it across the border into Euphoria, and we were saddened because we had to leave our homeland, Felicity, and

68

because we had lost the *Cryptolicity*. Then we saw our families and the priest waiting for us to enter the Royal Garden.

However, Prince James followed us to the border and waited for us to turn around; then he did the unspeakable. He shot us in the back with two silver arrows and flew back into Felicity. We were naive; we thought he got what he wanted. But we didn't know that he wanted revenge for his humiliation. That was when we held hands and said we would be back to fight a war against his people—to regain our right on Felicity. We swore on our true love that our souls would find one another during our next birth on my sixteenth birthday.

"After that we telepathically spoke our last words, 'I love you,' to one another and released our strengths and weaknesses, which were used to create the royal magic. We embraced and kissed for the last time, then fell onto the ground, smiling and looking at the light we had created—the same light that glowed around us when we kissed today. It was returning our strengths and weaknesses. We're now equipped to do our old magic, fight Prince Joshua, and get the *Cryptolicity* back. Blaze, they might have started the war back then and restarted it now, but this time we aren't going to leave anything unfinished. I love you."

Dear Diary:

I know it's been a while since I've written in you, a month to be exact; but I just haven't had any time. However, I figured out why I felt such a strong connection with Blaze. It turns out that the royal prophecy was written for us; we're the chosen two: the reincarnated Mimi Faylinn and Thomas 'Tommy' Eolande. He's my soul mate. Other than that, this past month has been very hectic. We've been training like crazy for the war. I learned some defensive and offensive skills using combination magic, which is a certain type of magic that only creatures with the Earth element can do. Surprisingly, I invented this kind of magic in my past life as Princess Mimi Faylinn.

Anyways, my defensive skill is done by combining the two elements of air and water to create a shield that protects people from silver. It doesn't let any kind of weapon come toward us, however, we can send out as many weapons as we want. Blaze taught me how to extend the shield so it protects all the citizens that are on the border. He knows how to do a shield that his father used to do,

70

but his is done with fire. Oh, and talking about fire: I also learned a skill done by combining air with fire, but it's a very dangerous offensive skill. Therefore, I'm going to just use it when I really need to. When I use this magic, it goes as far as I want and burns anything that I want into a little crisp, so it takes a lot of proper concentration and power to do it properly.

Blaze also taught me how to control the actions of other people—sort of how I controlled his actions on the first day of school. He's still the only person I can telepathically speak with, but now I can control the actions of Blaze, Warren, Drake, and Nixie. Which is good because once I take over their actions, my abilities start combining with theirs; in other words, Blaze taught me how to do combination magic using other peoples' magical powers. But, Diary, don't think that I'm the only one who learned something; Blaze learned offensive royal magic that he had created as Tommy Eolande. So now he can breathe out fire while still being in his human form, and he can create fire fists using his breath and hands. Once we combine our offensive skills, nothing can stand in our way. I just hope it'll help us with the war.

71

Mostly because Gramps is doing much worse now; he can't even get out of bed anymore. His face has started to go pale, and at times he forgets where he is and who the people around him are. Yesterday he kept asking where Grandma was, and when I explained that she had passed away, he asked me who I was.

We couldn't do anything to help him, and it was so depressing. But Papa Bear, my mom, and Rose all came for a little while to visit him. My Papa Bear did a spell on Rose's memory so she doesn't remember coming here at all. I'm actually quite frightened that Gramps is going to pass away soon, and I will become Queen Breena Faylinn. I mean, after all, I am only sixteen. Will I be able to run a country and handle a war? Not only that, but will I be able to keep Euphoria, the citizens, and the *Cryptoria* safe?

Sincerely,

Breena Faylinn

Chapter Nine:
The War Begins

❧

"PRINCESS, HURRY! IT'S KING FAYLINN! HE'S GASPING FOR AIR AND CALLING FOR YOU!" Yelled Madam V as everyone ran for the king's room.

This was it, the moment she didn't want to face. Her grandfather, King Faylinn was taking his last breaths.

"I love you, Breena. Take care of our kingdom; I trust that you and Blaze will make all of the royal ancestors proud. I just have one final request: would you please bury me in the garden beside my beautiful wife? I want to spend forever with her."

Breena couldn't believe it. Just like that, she was holding her grandfather's stone-cold corpse. Her worst nightmare had become a reality, but she knew that this was no time

73

to think about herself. She understood what she needed everyone to do.

"My Gramps is dead. We have to begin preparations for his funeral and a formal speech for our citizens. Drake and Nixie, I need both of you to go to my house and inform my parents to get here as soon as possible, preferably by tonight, and that's an order. We can't have the funeral without my father. Blaze, my lovely Prince, I need you and Warren to please work together for now and go to the border to find out how everything is going there. No matter what happens, everyone must remember to be back by seven thirty p.m."

Her grandfather was dead, and there was nothing she could do. Except, prepare a speech to let her people know what changes were going to happen.

She could hear a message coming from Blaze: "Princess, how are you doing? I just wanted to tell you that it's going alright on the border. Our men are making sure no one sneaks in. So we're coming back. Warren has talked to Drake as well; they told us to tell you that they're heading to the palace with your family."

74

Breena sat in her grandfather's bedroom and looked around; the room that was once filled with a joyful mood, now felt so heartbreaking. The walls that were always a nice, uplifting shade of purple had become a light gray color; the magic in the room was gone. Now all she could do was think about all her memories. This was where she had met her grandfather for the first time. It was the very place where she had promised to keep everyone safe by being the greatest queen that Euphoria had ever seen.

"Oh, darling, are you doing okay? Are you ready for the funeral and for everything else?" asked Eve as she ran into the room in tears.

All the people Breena loved were there now, which meant the funeral was about to take place.

They all went to the Royal Garden, where the current royal priest did a private ceremony, allowing friends and family to say their final good-byes to King Faylinn. A part of his last wish was fulfilled: he was buried beside his cherished wife.

And now it was time for Breena to get ready for the big ceremony. Eve, Nixie, and

75

Madam V started getting her dressed in a beautiful and elegant bluish-purple dress that matched her wings.

After she was fully dressed, Blaze came into her bedroom, pulled her closer by the waist, and gave her a kiss. Then he whispered in her ear, "Your voice makes my heart beat uncontrollably, your smile makes me want to be a better person, and your kiss makes my soul weak; you mean the world to me, and I promise that I will do anything to keep you safe. When I'm with you, I feel like I have the power to achieve anything. Breena Faylinn, you're my better half. I love you. That's why I'm placing this ring on your finger; it's to symbolize our undying love. May I have the honor of walking onto the balcony with Breena Faylinn, Queen of Euphoria?"

Breena couldn't stop her tears from flowing down her cheeks; she had fallen so deeply in love with Blaze. She didn't know how to express what was going on inside of her, but she was glad that he felt the same way. She looked at him and nodded as they made their way outside, as a royal couple.

Breena was surprised. She could see everyone that lived in Euphoria: the elves, the giants, the fairies, the guardian dragons,

76

and the pixies. They were all waiting to hear from her, their new queen. But before Breena started speaking, she was presented with her beautiful golden crown.

She looked up at the sky to take the blessings of her ancestors and then turned to her people. "I would like to thank all the citizens who have gathered here today. I would like to thank you for all the love you've given me during this difficult time. As everyone knows, my parents and sister live on Earth, and my grandfather has passed away; but that doesn't mean I'm alone; because all of you, the citizens of Euphoria, are my family and friends.

Therefore, we all have to be there for one another. I want the old to stay safe, the little ones to continue going to school, and everyone else to contribute in some way in keeping Euphoria safe. I know you must have heard that the war with Felicity has begun, which means that all of us need to keep a lookout. Please report any strangers or odd activity to me, Blaze, or anyone else associated with the royal families. I need everyone to make sure that they don't use their magic for useless things. I'm saying this because some of the members of Felicity have similar skills to our citizens, enabling them to steal the magic of others.

I hope everyone understands what we have to do; we have to fight Felicity and win back what was originally ours. We must beat King Joshua and gain the *Cryptolicity*; let us be combined as a single power and defeat their negative impact. Let the war begin."

Blaze and Breena both viewed all the citizens cheering. Then they smiled at one another knowing their past as Mimi and Tommy, knowing their goals, and knowing what they had to do. Lastly, the two royals held hands and yelled:

"God Bless Euphoria!"

Made in the USA
Charleston, SC
07 May 2013